MW00880514

Poems for the
Smart, Spunky, and
Sensational
Black Girl

Poems by: Rachel Garlinghouse
Illustrations by: Sharee Miller

Dear Reader,

My name is Rachel, and I'm a mom of three and writer. I've authored many articles and books, and one I'm most proud of is *Black Girls Can: An Empowering Story of Yesterdays and Todays*. This was the book I based "What If?" on.

The poems in this book were inspired by my children: in observations they've shared and situations they've experienced. I also include pieces of Black history, tidbits my children have learned. These poems are their truths. I'm honored to be the person putting the poems to paper to be shared with other children and their parents, teachers, caregivers, relatives, and friends.

Just like my children, you have so much to offer the world. You have pearls of insight, seeds of strength, and droplets of possibility. You are a unique jewel. You were fearfully and wonderfully made (Psalm 139:14) by the Almighty.

I hope the words and pictures in this book make you smile and remind you of just how incredible you are.

Love,
Rachel, mom of Miss A, Miss E, and Mr. I

Acknowledgements from Rachel

I'd like to thank Denene Millner (MyBrownBaby.com) for introducing me to Sharee's artwork. Denene has been such an encouragement to me over the past few years. Her wisdom, beauty, and determination are incredibly inspiring.

Thanks to Sharee Miller for her time and talent. This book is beautiful because of her! I'm so blessed to have found someone who was able to so perfectly turn my words into pictures.

Thanks to Mandan Kirk for doing the interior design, making this book an attractive and fun read for girls all over the world.

Thanks to Jennifer Buchanan for brainstorming with me on the book, including the SENSATIONAL title.

Finally, thank you to my children; they are my inspiration.

About

Rachel Garlinghouse is a former college writing teacher turned stay-at-home-mom and writer. Her work and experiences have been shared by MSNBC, NPR, Huffington Post, MyBrown-Baby.com, Huffington Post Live, Scary Mommy, Babble, Yahoo News, The Mighty, abcnews.com, Essence magazine, Adoptive Families, Medium, Fatherly, and many more. Rachel and her three children enjoy kitchen dance parties, creating art, visiting the library, and playing outdoors. Learn more about her family's adventures, link to her publications, and connect with her on social media by visiting www.whitesugarbrownsugar.com.

Sharee Miller has loved art all her life and has taken every opportunity to study it. In 2012 she earned her BFA in Communication Design from Pratt Institute. She now works in New York City as a freelance illustrator for children's books and as a graphic designer. She's the author and illustrator of *Princess Hair* and *Night Time Routine*, two books that inspire and promote love of one's natural hair. Sharee loves watching TV with her cat, traveling, and eating French fries. Follow Sharee on Instagram: @coilyandcute.

The Things
I Like
(for my E)

Everyone thinks I like princesses
And the color pink.
But they are wrong.
Everyone thinks I like ballet
And ruffles and sparkles.
But they are wrong.
Everyone thinks I like cupcakes
And skirts and fairies.
But they are wrong.
I like alligators
Capes
Basketball.
I like spooky stories
Hip hop dancing
New sneakers.
I like French fries dipped
Mud puddles
The color green.
I like swinging high
Dragons
And playing tag.
I am me.

What If?

What if Madam CJ Walker never would have created?

What if Bessie Coleman never would have flown?

What if Marian Anderson never would have sang?

What if Rosa Parks never would have refused?

What if Ruby Bridges never would have prayed?

What if Shirley Chisholm never would have led?

What if Toni Morrison never would have written?

What if Oprah Winfrey never would have spoken?

What if Mae Jemison never would have explored?

What if Michelle Obama never would have inspired?

Sidewalk Chalk

My family is like the rainbow
I draw
On the sidewalk
With thick bold chalk.
Each arch depends upon the next
Creating vibrance
Hope
Joy
Possibility.
With each drag
Across bumpy gray
I create
Remind
and smile.

THE NEW KID

I'm not too sure about this new baby.
He cries.
He coos.
Everyone admires him.
Smiles.
Brings gifts.
"In a minute."
"Not now."
"Quiet! The baby is sleeping!"
They say to me.
This tiny thing wrapped in blue
is king.
I'm feeling small.
Ignored.
I go to my room
Slam the door
And plop on my bed.
I throw my stuffed animals.
I scribble in a coloring book.
I stare out the window.
I fall asleep.
I wake up to Mom rubbing my back.
"Do you want to hold the baby?" she asks.
I'm uncertain this is what I want,
But I follow her to the living room anyway.
Mom puts a pillow under my arm and says,
"Here's your baby brother."
She lays him very gently in my arms.
He's warm.
He smells sweet like milk.
He sleeps soundly.
I am careful.
I am quiet.
I am smiling.
He likes me.
He needs me.
I am his big sister.

The Spirit of Queens

I come from royalty.
Flowing through my veins is
Bravery.
Determination.
Resilience.
Power.
Fierceness.
I carry this spirit in me.
I let it radiate through my
Words
Actions
Choices
I honor the ones who went before me.
And I create new history each day.
Blossoming into the Queen I was born to be.

My Shade

The shade of my skin is a gift from God.

My smooth latte.

My dark chocolate bar.

My cool cookie dough.

My warm whole wheat bread.

It's a history.

It's a promise.

It's a gift.

Beads

They

Click

Clack

Dance around me as I jump and

And twirl

And swing

And slide

And swim

And somersault.

My beads demand you listen.

You see.

You know I am here.

Let No One Despise

The Bible says
Let no one
(LET NO ONE)
Despise your youth.
Great things bud from beginnings
And taking chances
And having faith.
Michaela DePrince
Mo'nae Davis
Ruby Bridges
Jamie Grace.
Gabby Douglas.
These girls got grit.
They don't let.
They create.
They command.
They strive.
They don't quit.
No one can despise,
Because despising doesn't happen
without one's permission.
Let no one.

My Name

My name is a melody.

It's sweet.

It's powerful.

It's me.

Beautiful, wonderful me.

Strong me.

Smart me.

Talented me.

My name

is a song you won't soon forget.

My Birthday

Today!
Today I turn seven.
SEVEN!
I leap from my bed
Run to the kitchen.
Dad is baking cake.
Strawberry! My favorite!
I sit at the table, my legs swinging under me.
I cannot sit still.
Is it 2:00 yet? I ask Dad.
No.
Not yet.
Nope.
Tick tock. Tick tock. Tick tock.
At 2:00, my friends come over.
Keisha, Emma, Zoe, and Trinity.
We jump on trampoline
I listen to "Happy Birthday,"
My grin wide.
I blow out seven candles
We eat BIG pieces of cake
Listen to my favorite songs
I open gifts
My friends go home.
I sit in my room
Surrounded by my new things
My feet dirty and happy.
I drift to sleep that night
My dreams filled with
Streamers
Songs
Salutations
Sweet sugar
Happiness.
I'm seven!
I'm seven!
I'm SEVEN!

My Favorite Outfit

Mom says it's time to get dressed.
I dash to my room,
Throw open my dresser drawers,
And put on my favorite outfit.
Cheetah skort.
Sparkly tee.
Purple scarf.
Striped knee socks.
Rainbow flats.
Heart barrettes.
I stand in front of the mirror,
Hands on my hips.
Fly.
Fierce.
Strong.
In this outfit,
I can do anything.

Watch Me

Tell me I cannot do something.

Shouldn't be someone.

Tell me I shouldn't enjoy that.

Or be like this.

Tell me I'm supposed to stay

Within the boundaries you constructed.

And I'll tell you,

"Watch me."

Watch me soar.

Watch me learn.

Watch me succeed.

Watch me embrace.

Watch me dance.

Watch me relish.

And while you are watching,

I'm loving my life.

Between Mama's Knees

Between Mama's knees
I tell her my dreams.
Dreams of starring in a show,
Sledding in freshly fallen snow.
As Mama combs and conditions,
As she parts, braids, and beads.
I tell her my fears.
I ask thoughtful questions like
"Where does God put the sun at night?"
I shout out silly words.
I ask when she'll be done.
I grow restless.
I sigh.
I giggle and wiggle.
We sing songs.
She speaks to me about my gifts.
My strengths.
And then, and then,
She says, "You are done."
I stand.
I stretch.
I skip the mirror.
And I admire my art.
Between mamas' knees
beauty is born.

GUM

Today my teacher gave us gum.
We've been good all week.
We must put it in our backpacks.
It's for home, teacher says.

My piece is purple.
Grape.
As soon as I get home,
I drop my backpack on the floor
Retrieve the gum
And unwrap it in five seconds.
Mom peers at me from the kitchen.
"What's that?"
I grin and tell her I got gum.
"Don't you get that in your hair,"
she warns.
I nod and start chewing.
Grapey goodness bursts.
I chew.
And chew.
And chew.

I try to blow a bubble like my dad does.
I try again and again and again.
"Ugh!" I cry out in frustration.
And just as I get ready to try again,
Purple flies out of my mouth
And onto the floor.
I burst into tears.
My gum!
Arms crossed,
I glare at that wad of gum.
I feel a tap on my shoulder,
And turn.
Mom is standing behind me,
Her hand extended.
Nestled in her soft palm
Is a stick of minty gum.
She smiles.
I smile.
I try again.

Sunday Morning

Stained glass and swaying choir.

Bellowing preacher and faithful congregants.

Hats and suits.

Hymnals and Bibles.

Collection plates and wooden pews.

Teary eyes and waving hands.

Amens and Hallelujahs.

Prayers and confessions.

Familiar and new.

Peace and hope.

Joy and renewal.

Reminders and revelations.

Standing and sitting.

Swaying and singing.

Verses and visions.

Promises and praises.

All swirl around me,

Rooted in yesterdays,

Growing toward tomorrows,

On Sunday morning.

I Bel

I believe in me.

I like me.

I LOVE me.

I can be anything.

A unicorn tamer.

A chocolate baker.

A doctor who heals.

A race car driver with wheels.

A teacher who guides.

A nurse who provides.

ieve

A surfer who rides.

A pilot who glides.

A politician who stands.

A rock star with fans.

A teammate with a ball.

A coach with a call.

I believe in me.

I like me.

I LOVE me.

My Santa

Smooth brown cheeks tinged pink.

White cotton-candy beard.

Rounded tummy full of homemade cookies.

Chocolatey, kind, mischievous eyes.

Tote lumpy with surprises.

Merry and magical.

Calm and bright.

Christmas Eve night.

First Day

I was restless last night
I hardly slept a wink
I was thinking about today
And summer's exit like a blink.
My pencils are sharpened.
My lunch is packed.
My folder is labeled.
My books are stacked.
I'm feeling a little nervous
I'm feeling a little sad
I'm hope I make new friends
I hope my teacher is glad.
The doors are propped open
The hallways are loud
The lockers are squeaking
The principal looks proud.
The classroom is bright
The teacher claps her hands
We quickly find our seats
Teacher tells us her plans.

of School

We learn about warnings
We learn the rules
We learn about lines
We are going to love school!
We listen to a story
We are assigned a seat
We play outside
We head to the cafeteria to eat.
I put together a puzzle with a friend
She was in my class last year
My teacher rewards us with a chocolate
We all let out a cheer!
Soon the clock strikes three
Time to pack up and head out
Mom asks how was school
I loved it, I shout!

The Girl on the Bus

Last week, a girl on the bus laughed at me
She sneered that my pink glasses were ugly
I was scared
She was older and mean
I tried to ignore her
She pecked at me like a chicken
Trying to steal my dignity
It happened again
And again
And again
One day, I couldn't hold it in anymore
I told my mama
I tried to cover my pain with a shaky smile
My mama, she's no fool
The next day, the girl made fun of me again
And I said to her, in a loud firm voice (like mama said to use)
That I was beautiful. I liked me. I liked my glasses
I told her to leave. me. alone
The girl looked stunned
I didn't drop my gaze
I let her see my strong brown eyes
through my pink frames
That girl. She didn't bother me again
And I kept on wearing my glasses

Saturday Blues

It's Saturday.

The day mom says the dreaded words.

Go clean your room.

"I don't want to!"

Pause. Wider eyes.

"No sass. Go."

I like my room messy.

I know exactly where my things are.

Well, sometimes.

Clothes, dolls, beads, markers

Make up a collage on my floor.

My bed is a tangle of

Sheets, quilt, stuffed bears.

My bookshelf contains

Books, pencils, a jump rope.

My dresser is spilling open with

Mismatched socks,

My old gymnastics leotards

And last summer's dresses.

There's a package of fruit snacks

A party favor bag

A straw.

My room is just how I like it!

I lay on top of the piles on my floor

Hands behind my head

And smile.

Slumber Party

Doorbell rings.

Shrieks and giggles.

Dashing off.

Sleeping bags and pillows.

Nailpolish and nightgowns.

Movies and popcorn.

Music and dancing.

Lights go out.

Lights go on.

"Shhhh," grownups warn.

Lights go out.

Ghost stories whispered.

Candy wrappers and flashlights.

Whispers and muffled laughter.

Sighs and snoring.

Stars twinkle.

Girls slumber.

At the
Beauty Shop

There's a hundred conversations.

Spinning chairs.

Foot tapping, shoulder swaying, head
nodding music.

There's ladies in lipstick.

Purses in seats.

Magazines on tables.

There's light from rounded bulbs.

Blow dryers.

Sizzling flat irons.

Sprays.

Creams.

Combs.

Polished fingernails.

Fast moving fingers.

Laughter.

Heads thrown back.

Memories shared.

News discussed.

Solidarity.

Disagreement.

Singing.

Mirrors.

Nods.

Admiration.

Unity.

Another day

Another memory made

At the beauty shop.

Sunglasses

When I wear my shades

I am a movie star.

A spy.

A princess in disguise.

I am a pop star.

A fashionista.

A superhero.

When I wear my shades

I am magic.

Made in the USA
San Bernardino, CA
06 December 2016